A CONTEMPORARY ROMANCE SERIES

*Series Guide*

*Melissa Foster*

ISBN-13: 978-1-941480-21-2
ISBN-10: 1941480217

Cover Design: ELIZABETH MACKEY

WORLD LITERARY PRESS
PRINTED IN THE UNITED STATES OF AMERICA

# A Note to Readers

Your love of our hot, sexy, and wickedly naughty Love in Bloom heroes and heroines inspires me on a daily basis. I hope this guide is valuable to you as we watch these lovable characters fall in love, marry, and have families of their own. Be sure to sign up for my newsletter so you never miss a release!

Please note: Age noted for characters reflect their current age at the time *their* story took place.

*Melissa Foster*

NEWSLETTER:
http://www.melissafoster.com/newsletter

## CONNECT WITH MELISSA

TWITTER:
https://twitter.com/Melissa_Foster

FACEBOOK:
https://www.facebook.com/MelissaFosterAuthor

WEBSITE:
http://www.melissafoster.com

STREET TEAM:
http://www.facebook.com/groups/melissafosterfans

*Melissa Foster*

*For my readers
and with much heartfelt gratitude to my favorite diva,
Michelle Garrett, without whom
this guide would not be as awesome!*

# FAMILY TREE

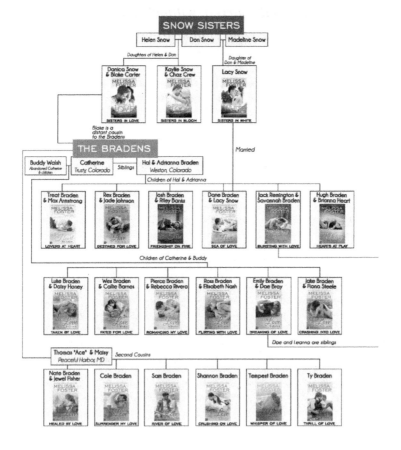

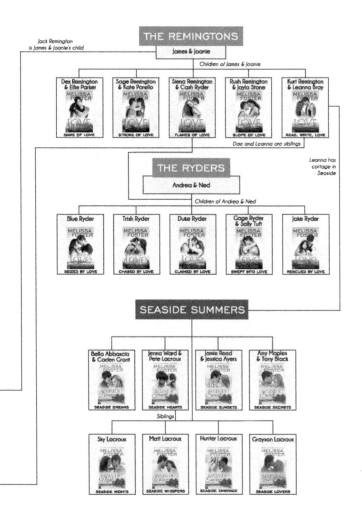

THE REMINGTONS

James & Joanie

Jack Remington
is James & Joanie's child

Children of James & Joanie

| Dex Remington & Elite Parker | Sage Remington & Kate Parello | Siena Remington & Cash Ryder | Rush Remington & Jayla Stone | Kurt Remington & Leanna Bray |
|---|---|---|---|---|
| GAME OF LOVE | STROKE OF LOVE | FLAMES OF LOVE | SLOPE OF LOVE | READ, WRITE, LOVE |

Dae and Leanna are siblings

Leanna has cottage in Seaside

THE RYDERS

Andrea & Ned

Children of Andrea & Ned

| Blue Ryder | Trish Ryder | Duke Ryder | Gage Ryder & Sally Tuft | Jake Ryder |
|---|---|---|---|---|
| SEIZED BY LOVE | CHASED BY LOVE | CLAIMED BY LOVE | SWEPT INTO LOVE | RESCUED BY LOVE |

SEASIDE SUMMERS

| Bella Abbascia & Caden Grant | Jenna Ward & Pete Lacroux | Jamie Reed & Jessica Ayers | Amy Maples & Tony Black |
|---|---|---|---|
| SEASIDE DREAMS | SEASIDE HEARTS | SEASIDE SUNSETS | SEASIDE SECRETS |

Siblings

| Sky Lacroux | Matt Lacroux | Hunter Lacroux | Grayson Lacroux |
|---|---|---|---|
| SEASIDE NIGHTS | SEASIDE WHISPERS | SEASIDE EMBRACE | SEASIDE LOVERS |

*NEW YORK TIMES* BESTSELLING AUTHOR

# MELISSA FOSTER

NEW YORK TIMES BESTSELLING AUTHOR

# MELISSA FOSTER

# SISTERS IN LOVE

{ SNOW SISTERS }

LOVE IN BLOOM SERIES BOOK ONE

CONTEMPORARY ROMANCE

Danica Snow has always been the smart, practical, and appropriate sister. As a therapist, she prides herself on making reasonable, conservative choices, even if a bit boring, and as part of the Big Sister Program, she has little time for anything more in her life.

Blake Carter is a player. He never gets bored of conquering women, and with his sexy good looks and successful lifestyle, he has no trouble finding willing participants. When his friend and business partner dies in a tragic accident, he suddenly, desperately, wants to change his ways. The problem is, he doesn't know how to stop doing what he does best.

When Blake walks into Danica's office, the attraction between them is white hot, but Danica isn't the type to give into the heat and risk her career. Danica's desire sets her on a path of self-discovery, where she begins to question every decision she's ever made. Just this once, Danica wants to indulge in the pleasures of life she's been so willingly ignoring, but with her Little Sister in turmoil and her biological sister's promiscuousness weighing heavily on her heart, she isn't sure it's the right time to set her desires free.

### *Sisters in Love*, Snow Sisters, Book 1
### **Setting**: Allure, Colorado

### **Danica Snow**
Therapist
Blue eyes, brown curly hair
29

### **SIBLINGS**
Kaylie, Lacy
(half sister, father's side)

### **PARENTS**
Don & Helen Snow
(divorced)
Madeline Snow (stepmother)

### **Blake Carter**
Owner of AcroSki
Green eyes, black hair
34

### **PARENTS**
Harry Carter

## CHILDREN

_____

_____

_____

_____

## BOOK ENGAGED

_____

## BOOK MARRIED

_____

## PETS

_____

## OTHER NOTES

_____

_____

_____

_____

NEW YORK TIMES BESTSELLING AUTHOR

# MELISSA FOSTER

## SISTERS IN BLOOM

{ SNOW SISTERS }

LOVE IN BLOOM SERIES BOOK TWO

CONTEMPORARY ROMANCE

Kaylie Snow has always been the fun, flirty, pretty sister. Now her burgeoning baby bump, hormone-infused emotions, and faltering singing career are sending her into an unexpected identity crisis. Watching her older sister, Danica, glide through a major career change and a new relationship with the grace of a ballerina, Kaylie's insecurities rise to the forefront—and her relationship with fiancé Chaz Crew is caught in the crossfire.

Chaz Crew has everything he's ever wanted: a lovely fiancée, a baby on the way, and soon, the film festival he owns will host its biggest event ever. When he's called away to woo the festival's largest sponsor—and the lover he's never admitted to having—secrets from his past turn his new life upside down.

With her baby shower around the corner and her fiancé's big event looming, the pressure is on for Kaylie to pull herself together—and for Chaz to right his wrongs. In a few short weeks, the couple who had it all figured out will learn things about life and love that may change their minds—and their hearts.

**Sisters in Bloom**, Snow Sisters, Book 2
**Setting**: Allure, Colorado

**Kaylie Snow**
Singer
Blue eyes, blond hair
27

**SIBLINGS**
Danica, Lacy
(half sister, father's side)

**PARENTS**
Don & Helen Snow
(divorced)
Madeline Snow (stepmother)

**Chaz Crew**
Owner of Indie Film Festival
Blue eyes, blond hair

**SIBLINGS**
Weston, Astrid, Abby

**PARENTS**
Elise Crew

*Melissa Foster*

## CHILDREN

_____

_____

_____

_____

## BOOK ENGAGED

_____

## BOOK MARRIED

_____

## PETS

_____

## OTHER NOTES

_____

_____

_____

_____

_____

NEW YORK TIMES BESTSELLING AUTHOR

# MELISSA FOSTER

## SISTERS IN WHITE

{ SNOW SISTERS }

LOVE IN BLOOM SERIES BOOK THREE

CONTEMPORARY ROMANCE

Danica and Kaylie Snow are about to celebrate the biggest day of their lives—their double wedding—on an island in the Bahamas. But no wedding is complete without a little family drama. The two sisters aren't ready to face the father they haven't seen since he divorced their mother and moved away to marry his mistress, and live with Lacy, the half sister they've never met.

While Danica has exchanged letters and phone calls with Lacy, Kaylie has fervently tried to pretend she doesn't exist. Lacy is sweet, fun, and nearly a mirror image of Kaylie. To make matters worse, not only is Lacy looking forward to meeting her sisters, but she idolizes them, too. As the countdown to the wedding date ticks on, their parents are playing a devious game of revenge, and there's a storm brewing over the island, threatening to cancel their perfect wedding. The sisters are about to find out if the bond of sisterhood really trumps all.

***Sisters in White***, Snow Sisters, Book 3
**Setting**: Nassau, Bahamas

## Same heroes and heroines as Sisters in Love & Sisters in Bloom

## READER NOTES

_____

_____

_____

_____

_____

_____

_____

_____

_____

_____

_____

_____

_____

_____

## CHILDREN

_____

_____

_____

## FUN FACTS

_____

## OTHER FAMILY INFO

_____

## PETS

_____

## OTHER NOTES

_____

_____

_____

_____

_____

NEW YORK TIMES BESTSELLING AUTHOR

# MELISSA FOSTER

"Sensual, sexy, and satisfying."
Bestselling author, Keri Nola, LMHC

## Lovers at *Heart*

### The Bradens

Book One: Love in Bloom Series

Handsome, wealthy resort owner Treat Braden is used to getting what he wants. When Max Armstrong walked into his life six months earlier, he saw right through the efficient and capable façade she wore like a shield, to the sweet, sensual woman who lay beneath. She sparked an unfamiliar desire in him for more than a one-night stand, leaving his heart reeling and his blood boiling. But one mistake caused her to turn away, and now, after six months of longing for the one woman he cannot have, he's going home to try to forget her all together.

Max Armstrong has a successful career, a comfortable lifestyle, and she's never needed a man to help her find her way—until Treat Braden caught her attention at a wedding in Nassau, causing a surge of emotions too reminiscent of the painful past she'd spent years trying to forget. Max will do anything to avoid reliving that pain—including forgoing her toe-curling, heart-pounding desire for Treat.

When a chance encounter turns into a night of intense passion, Treat realizes that the mistake he made six months earlier may cause him to lose Max completely. He will do everything within his power to win her heart forever—and Max is forced to face her hurtful past head on for the man she cannot help but love.

***Lovers at Heart***, The Bradens (Weston, CO), Book 1
**Setting**: Allure & Weston, Colorado;
Wellfleet, Massachusetts

**Max Armstrong**
Sponsor Coordinator of
Indie Film Festival
Hazel eyes, wavy brown hair
28

**Treat Braden**
Resort Owner
Dark eyes, thick dark hair
37

**SIBLINGS**
Dane, Rex, Savannah,
Josh, Hugh

**PARENTS**
Hal & Adriana Braden
(mother deceased)

## CHILDREN

_____

_____

_____

_____

## BOOK ENGAGED

_____

## BOOK MARRIED

_____

## PETS

_____

## OTHER NOTES

_____

_____

_____

_____

_____

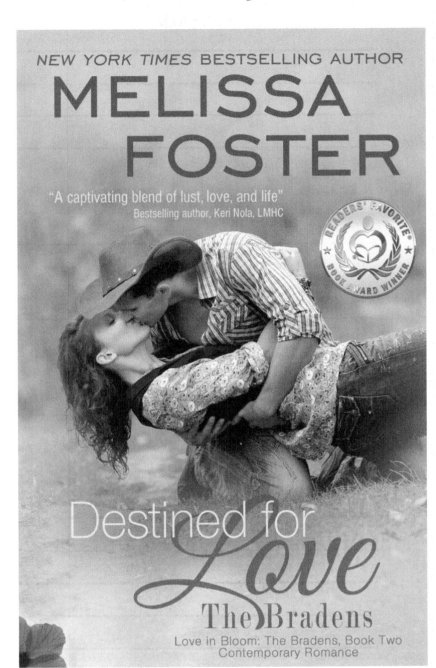

NEW YORK TIMES BESTSELLING AUTHOR

# MELISSA FOSTER

"A captivating blend of lust, love, and life"
Bestselling author, Keri Nola, LMHC

READERS' FAVORITE
BOOK AWARD WINNER

Destined for
*Love*

The Bradens

Love in Bloom: The Bradens, Book Two
Contemporary Romance

Rex Braden is wealthy, hardworking, and fiercely loyal. Sweat at his brow, he works the family ranch by day, then kicks back at night with part time lovers who require nothing more than his physical presence a few times each month. But that was before. Before Jade Johnson, the daughter of the man his father has been feuding with for over forty years, moves back into town.

After ditching a horrific relationship—and her veterinary practice in the process—Jade Johnson returns to the safety of her small hometown and finally finds her footing. That is...until her horse is injured and Rex Braden comes to her rescue. The last thing she needs is a bull-headed, too-handsome-for-his-own-good Braden complicating her life.

Despite the angry family history, sparks fly between Rex and Jade, and attitudes follow. Fifteen years of stifled, forbidden love stirs a surge of passion too strong for either to deny—and the rebel in each of them rears its powerful head. Loyalties are tested, and relationships are strained. Rex and Jade are about to find out if true love really can conquer all.

***Destined for Love***, The Bradens (Weston, CO), Book 2
**Setting**: Weston, Colorado

**Jade Johnson**
Veterinarian;
Equine Therapist
Blue eyes, long black hair
31

**SIBLINGS**
Steven

**PARENTS**
Earl & Jane Johnson

**Rex Braden**
Rancher
Dark eyes, thick dark hair
34

**SIBLINGS**
Treat, Dane, Savannah,
Josh, Hugh

**PARENTS**
Hal & Adriana Braden
(mother deceased)

**CHILDREN**

_____

_____

_____

_____

**BOOK ENGAGED**

_____

**BOOK MARRIED**

_____

**PETS**

_____

**OTHER NOTES**

_____

_____

_____

_____

_____

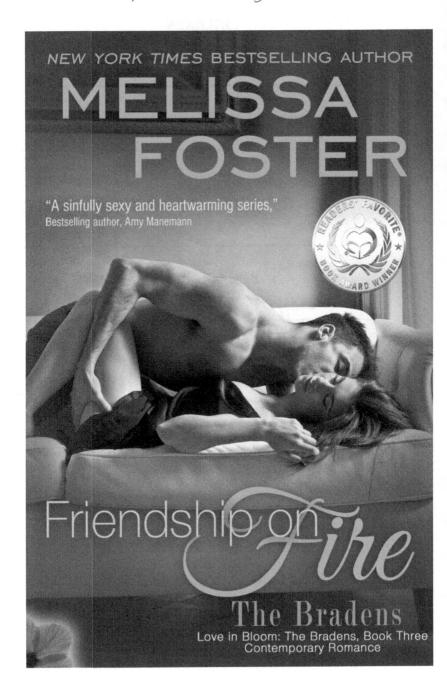

NEW YORK TIMES BESTSELLING AUTHOR

# MELISSA FOSTER

"A sinfully sexy and heartwarming series,"
Bestselling author, Amy Manemann

## Friendship on Fire

### The Bradens

Love in Bloom: The Bradens, Book Three
Contemporary Romance

Small-town overachiever Riley Banks has finally scored her big break—working in Manhattan as a fashion design assistant for her childhood crush, Josh Braden. She enters her new job hoping to make a name for herself and—just maybe—explore the romance that slipped through her fingers way back when.

Josh Braden has models at his beck and call, a staff that never says never, and an elegant clothing line for the holiday season. When he hires Riley Banks, he expects her to learn the business from the ground up. But the girl next door turns out to be much more than he remembered.

Josh and Riley's friendship heats up. Every steamy kiss and every erotic caress stirs a love they cannot deny. But when Riley designs a wedding gown that would cause even the most jaded fashion editors to swoon, Riley's mentor accuses her of stealing the design.

Facing indisputable proof and the mistrust of her lover, Riley is not sure she can take the heat of life in the fast lane of the fashion industry—and Josh is forced to choose between the woman he loves and the career he adores.

***Friendship on Fire***, The Bradens (Weston, CO), Book 3
**Setting**: Manhattan, New York

### Riley Banks
Fashion Design Assistant
Hazel eyes, brunette
31

### PARENTS
Arlene Banks

### Josh Braden
Fashion Designer
Brown eyes, thick dark hair
33

### SIBLINGS
Treat, Dane, Rex,
Savannah, Hugh

### PARENTS
Hal & Adriana Braden
(mother deceased)

## CHILDREN

_____

_____

_____

_____

## BOOK ENGAGED

_____

## BOOK MARRIED

_____

## PETS

_____

## OTHER NOTES

_____

_____

_____

_____

_____

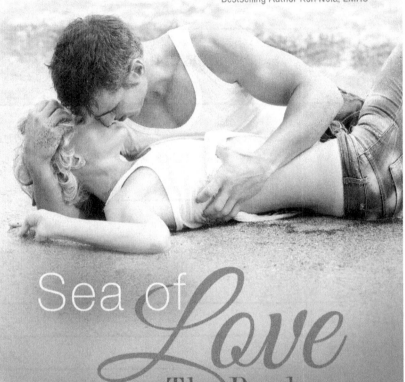

NEW YORK TIMES BESTSELLING AUTHOR

# MELISSA FOSTER

"A passionate and romantic exploration
of fear and love."
Bestselling Author Keri Nola, LMHC

Sea of *Love*

The Bradens
Book Four: Love in Bloom Series

Lacy Snow wasn't looking for love when she met strikingly handsome and seductive Dane Braden. But how could she ignore the six-foot-three darkly handsome god who tagged and researched sharks for a living—and made every nerve in her body tangle into an overly sensitive knot? Even her fear of sharks could not suppress their intense attraction.

As founder of the Brave Foundation, Dane Braden travels from port to port, educating and advocating on behalf of the mammals he adores—and spends his nights finding solace in the arms of strangers. The last thing Dane was looking for when he met Lacy Snow was a relationship, and the last thing he expected was to fall in love.

Fifteen months—and hundreds of flirty emails, steamy phone calls, and sensual video chats—later, they reunite and take passion to a whole new level. But as Lacy's phobia meets Dane's past love life, their steamy romance is upended, and when tragedy strikes, Dane and Lacy are forced to face their deepest fears head-on as they try to navigate their own sea of love.

***Sea of Love***, The Bradens (Weston, CO), Book 4
**Setting**: Wellfleet and Chatham, Massachusetts

**Lacy Snow**
Senior Advertising Executive at
World Geographic
Blue eyes, curly blond hair
27

**SIBLINGS**
Danica, Kaylie,
(half sisters, father's side)

**PARENTS**
Don & Madeline Snow

**Dane Braden**
Founder of
Brave Foundation;
Shark Tagger
Dark brown eyes, dark hair
36

**SIBLINGS**
Treat, Rex, Savannah,
Josh, Hugh

**PARENTS**
Hal & Adriana Braden
(mother deceased)

## CHILDREN

_____

_____

_____

_____

## BOOK ENGAGED

_____

## BOOK MARRIED

_____

## PETS

_____

## OTHER NOTES

_____

_____

_____

_____

_____

NEW YORK TIMES BESTSELLING AUTHOR

# MELISSA FOSTER

## Bursting with Love

### The Bradens

Love in Bloom: The Bradens, Book Five
Contemporary Romance

After having her heart broken by a country music star, Savannah Braden has sworn off men. She takes a break from her fast-paced Manhattan lifestyle for a weekend at a survivor camp to rebuild her confidence and readjust her priorities. But when she meets the handsome guide, Jack Remington, she's drawn to everything about him—from his powerful physique to his brooding stare—despite the big chip on his shoulder. Powerless to ignore the heated glances and mounting sexual tension, Savannah begins to reassess her hasty decision.

After losing his wife in a tragic accident, Jack Remington found solace in the Colorado Mountains. This solitary existence allows him to wallow in his guilt and punish himself for having made a decision that he believes cost his wife her life. He never expected to want to return to the life he once knew— but then again, he never expected to meet gorgeous, stubborn, and competitive Savannah Braden.

One passionate kiss is all it takes to crack the walls the two have built to protect themselves, and allow love to slip in. While Jack fights his way through his guilt, and struggles to get back into the lives of those he left behind, Savannah is there to help him heal, and together they nurture hope that they've finally found their forever loves.

***Bursting with Love***, The Bradens (Weston, CO), Book 5
**Setting**: Colorado Mountains; Manhattan, New York

### Savannah Braden
Entertainment Attorney
Hazel eyes, long auburn hair
34

### SIBLINGS
Treat, Dane, Rex, Josh, Hugh

### PARENTS
Hal & Adriana Braden
(mother deceased)

### Jack Remington
Survival Guide
Blue eyes, wavy brown hair
37

### SIBLINGS
Rush, Kurt,
Sage, Dex, Siena

### PARENTS
James & Joanie Remington

## CHILDREN

_____

_____

_____

_____

## BOOK ENGAGED

_____

## BOOK MARRIED

_____

## PETS

_____

## OTHER NOTES

_____

_____

_____

_____

_____

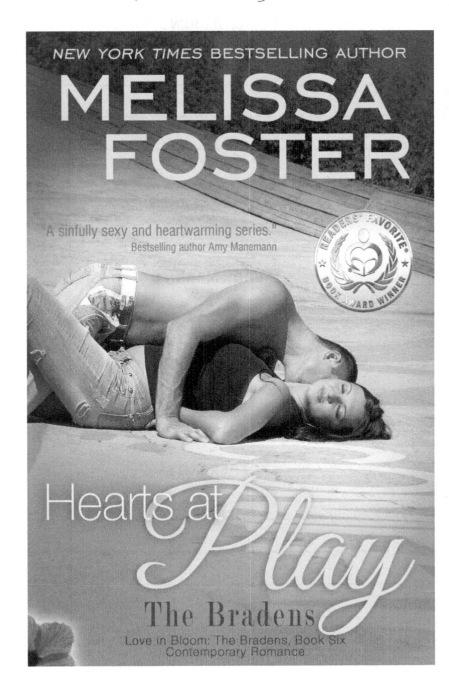

NEW YORK TIMES BESTSELLING AUTHOR

# MELISSA FOSTER

"A sinfully sexy and heartwarming series."
Bestselling author Amy Manemann

READERS' FAVORITE
BOOK AWARD WINNER

Hearts at Play

The Bradens

Love in Bloom: The Bradens, Book Six
Contemporary Romance

Brianna Heart has a six-year-old daughter and a twelve-year plan to keep her life as simple as possible until Layla turns eighteen. That means swearing off relationships and the drama that goes along with them, working two jobs, and being the best damn mother she can be.

The last thing Capital Series Grand Prix racer Hugh Braden wants after dating media-hungry leggy models and money-hungry fan girls is a blind date. But how could he turn down a favor to one of his best friends? Hugh expected the date to go poorly, but he didn't expect to be intensely attracted to the beautiful brown-eyed bartender who completely blows him off—and steals his every thought thereafter.

When Brianna's perfectly orchestrated life turns upside down, Hugh is there to help, softening the turmoil, and maybe even rescuing her heart from the lonely place where it has been hiding. Can a man who doesn't believe in fate and a woman who doesn't believe in true love find happiness in each other's arms forever?

**_Hearts at Play_**, The Bradens (Weston, CO), Book 6
**Setting**: Richmond, Virginia

**Brianna Heart**
Waitress
Brown eyes, brown hair
28

**PARENTS**
Jean Heart

**Hugh Braden**
Race Car Driver
Cocoa-brown eyes, black hair
29

**SIBLINGS**
Treat, Dane, Rex,
Savannah, Josh

**PARENTS**
Hal & Adriana Braden
(mother deceased)

## CHILDREN
Layla, age 6 (Brianna's daughter)

## BOOK ENGAGED

## BOOK MARRIED

## PETS

## OTHER NOTES

NEW YORK TIMES BESTSELLING AUTHOR

# MELISSA FOSTER

Taken by *Love*

## The Bradens

Love in Bloom: The Bradens
Contemporary Romance

Daisy Honey fled Trusty, Colorado, after years of battling rumors sparked by her gorgeous looks and lust-inducing name. Now a physician on the brink of a promising career, she reluctantly returns home when her father is injured in a farming accident. Daisy expects the small-town girls who hurt her in the past to take cheap shots again—but she's completely unprepared for a run-in with tall, dark, and wickedly sexy Luke Braden, the only man who has ever stood up for her—and the man she's never forgotten.

Luke Braden is handsome, wealthy, and the best damn gypsy horse breeder in the Midwest. After a restless youth, he's finally ready to settle down—only connecting with women is nothing like connecting with horses, and he's never met a woman worth the energy. After an arrest in a neighboring town, Luke's past comes back to haunt him, and he realizes that his inability to find love runs deeper than he ever imagined.

A chance encounter sweeps Luke and Daisy into a world of passion. For the first time ever, Luke feels a connection, but Daisy's life in Trusty is anything but permanent, and Luke can't manage a future until he puts his past to rest.

**Taken by Love**, The Bradens (Trusty, CO), Book 7
**Setting**: Trusty, Colorado

**Daisy Honey**
Physician
Blue eyes, blond hair
29

**PARENTS**
David & Susan Honey

**Luke Braden**
Gypsy Horse Breeder
Dark eyes, dark hair
30

**SIBLINGS**
Pierce, Ross, Jake,
Wes, Emily

**PARENTS**
Catherine Braden
Buddy Walsh
(deserted family)

## CHILDREN

_____

_____

_____

_____

## BOOK ENGAGED

_____

## BOOK MARRIED

_____

## PETS

_____

## OTHER NOTES

_____

_____

_____

_____

_____

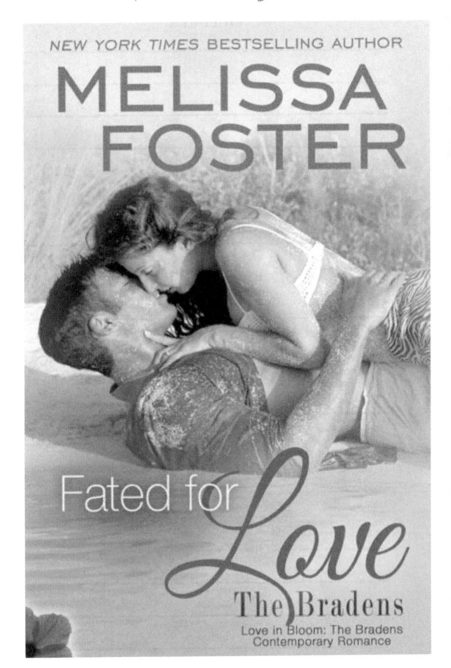

NEW YORK TIMES BESTSELLING AUTHOR

# MELISSA FOSTER

Fated for *Love*

## The Bradens

Love in Bloom: The Bradens
Contemporary Romance

Librarian Callie Barnes has visions of reading and relaxing—and maybe having a few too many drinks—on her girls' weekend away. Her hopes are crushed when her friends pull into a dude ranch instead of a spa, and she refuses to stay longer than one night. That is...until she realizes the ranch is owned by sinfully sexy, and dangerously rugged, Wes Braden—the subject of her late-night fantasies.

Fearless rancher Wes Braden thinks he's the luckiest guy on the planet when the sweet, sexy librarian from his hometown shows up at his ranch. Their connection is white-hot, making it impossible for either to ignore their carnal desires. Wes is more than willing to convert sweet Callie from chick lit to a world of erotic romance, but Callie ties sex to love, and Wes avoids commitment like the plague.

Callie is thrust into physically demanding activities that ignite her deepest fears. Luckily, Wes is as tender as he is strong, and he's there every step of the way to help her find her inner strength. With Callie's influence, Wes might even discover that he's been nursing a few fears of his own. Passion pulls Callie and Wes from their safe, comfortable lives into each other's arms, and they're about to find out just how alike they really are.

*Fated for Love*, The Bradens (Trusty, CO), Book 8
**Setting**: The Woodlands Dude Ranch (Colorado)

**Callie Barnes**
Librarian
Brown eyes, brunette
26

**Wes Braden**
Co-Owner of
The Woodlands Dude Ranch
Piercing dark eyes, dark hair
32

**SIBLINGS**
Pierce, Ross, Jake,
Emily, Luke

**PARENTS**
Catherine Braden
Buddy Walsh
(deserted family)

*Melissa Foster*

## CHILDREN

---

---

---

---

## BOOK ENGAGED

---

## BOOK MARRIED

---

## PETS

---

## OTHER NOTES

---

---

---

---

---

NEW YORK TIMES BESTSELLING AUTHOR

# MELISSA FOSTER

Romancing My
*Love*

The Bradens

Love in Bloom: The Bradens
Contemporary Romance

After months of caring for her terminally ill mother, Rebecca Rivera is left all alone in a world she doesn't trust—but she's determined not to let her mother's death define her. Losing her job, having to pummel some jerk for being too handsy, and living in her car are just temporary setbacks to an otherwise solid plan in finding her footing. Full of pride and used to being in control of her life, she's certain she can make it on her own. The last thing Rebecca needs is a man to fix her troubles— even if that man is strikingly handsome, wealthy, and charismatic Pierce Braden.

Pierce is a powerful real estate investor and casino owner on the verge of a major acquisition. As the eldest of six siblings raised by a single mother, he's spent his life protecting those he loves. He's used to being in charge and making things right, and although he'd give his life for his family, he treats the women he dates as expendable—until he meets sexy and stubborn Rebecca Rivera, a woman who is as strong as she is vulnerable.

Passion ignites between them, and the two share their most intimate thoughts and desires. It doesn't take long for Pierce to realize that Rebecca is as determined not to be saved as he is to find a way into her heart. As their love grows, Rebecca must face fears she didn't even realize she had—and Pierce must learn the hard truth that sometimes less really is more. Is the power of true love enough for Rebecca and Pierce to learn to give up control and allow their hearts to take over?

**Romancing My Love**, The Bradens (Trusty, CO), Book 9
**Setting**: Reno, Nevada

**Rebecca Rivera**
Waitress
Dark eyes, brunette
27

**PARENTS**
Magda Rivera (deceased)

**Pierce Braden**
Real Estate Investor &
Casino Owner
Dark eyes, dark hair
36

**SIBLINGS**
Ross, Jake,
Wes, Emily, Luke

**PARENTS**
Catherine Braden
Buddy Walsh (deserted family)

## CHILDREN

_____

_____

_____

_____

## BOOK ENGAGED

_____

## BOOK MARRIED

_____

## PETS

_____

## OTHER NOTES

_____

_____

_____

_____

_____

NEW YORK TIMES BESTSELLING AUTHOR

# MELISSA FOSTER

Flirting with

*Love*

## The Bradens

Love in Bloom: The Bradens
Contemporary Romance

Elisabeth Nash has spent years dreaming of returning to the small town of Trusty, Colorado, where she spent summers with her favorite aunt. When she inherits her aunt's farmette, she closes her Los Angeles pet bakery and pampering business, sure that life in Trusty will be as peaceful and as welcoming as she remembers. But being an outsider in the close-knit town proves to be very different from the happy summers she remembers from her childhood—and falling for Trusty's hot, wealthy, and sinfully irresistible veterinarian, Ross Braden, sends the rumor mill into a frenzy.

Ross Braden learned long ago that gossip spreads faster than weeds in his small hometown, and Ross loves nothing more than his privacy. For that reason, he doesn't date women who live in Trusty. But that was before blonde, beautiful, and refreshingly honest Elisabeth Nash flew into his vet clinic seeking help for her panicked piglet and turned his comfortable life—and his heart—inside out.

Despite rumors about Elisabeth's motives toward her aunt's property, passion brews between Elisabeth and Ross. Every steamy kiss and every sensual touch brings the pair closer together, and when Ross helps Elisabeth try to fit into the town he adores, it makes their bond even stronger. But even Elisabeth's efforts toward reaching the community, and the love she and Ross so desperately believe in, might not be enough for the protective small town to offer them a future.

***Flirting with Love***, The Bradens (Trusty, CO), Book 10
**Setting**: Trusty, Colorado

**Elisabeth Nash**
Owner of
Trusty Pies & Pet Pampering
Green eyes, blond hair
27

**Ross Braden**
Veterinarian
Dark eyes, dark hair
35

**SIBLINGS**
Pierce, Jake,
Wes, Emily, Luke

**PARENTS**
Catherine Braden
Buddy Walsh
(deserted family)

*Melissa Foster*

## CHILDREN

_____

_____

_____

_____

## BOOK ENGAGED

_____

## BOOK MARRIED

_____

## PETS

_____

## OTHER NOTES

_____

_____

_____

_____

_____

NEW YORK TIMES BESTSELLING AUTHOR

# MELISSA FOSTER

Dreaming of

*Love*

## The Bradens

Love in Bloom: The Bradens
Contemporary Romance

Emily Braden is a leader in architectural preservation, a pillar in her small hometown, and successful in everything she does—with the exception of finding true love. She's watched several of her brothers fall in love, and she needs this trip to Tuscany to get away from it all and to stop focusing on what she doesn't have.

Dae Bray doesn't do flings, and he never stays in one place for very long. As a demolitionist, he goes where jobs take him, and the more often he travels, the better. His trip to Tuscany is all work—until he meets smart and sexy Emily, who makes him reconsider his fear of settling down, his no-fling rule—and just about everything else he's ever believed about himself.

Passion sizzles as Dae and Emily explore the history and beauty of Tuscany. Their romance moves beyond tourist attractions to the bedroom, blossoming into a deep connection neither can deny. But their worlds collide when Emily wants to preserve the property that Dae is there to demolish. Can a woman who sees the beauty in preservation and a man whose life is spent tearing things down find a solid foundation for their love?

## *Dreaming of Love*, The Bradens (Trusty, CO), Book 11
### Setting: Tuscany, Italy

**Emily Braden**
Passive Home Architect
Dark eyes, long brown hair
31

**SIBLINGS**
Pierce, Ross, Jake,
Wes, Luke

**PARENTS**
Catherine Braden
Buddy Walsh
(deserted family)

**Dae Bray**
Demolition Expert
Brown eyes, brown hair

**SIBLINGS**
Leanna, Colby,
Wade, Bailey

**PARENTS**
Will & Gina Bray

*Melissa Foster*

## CHILDREN

_____

_____

_____

_____

## BOOK ENGAGED

_____

## BOOK MARRIED

_____

## PETS

_____

## OTHER NOTES

_____

_____

_____

_____

_____

NEW YORK TIMES BESTSELLING AUTHOR

# MELISSA FOSTER

## Crashing into *Love*

### The Bradens

Love in Bloom: The Bradens
Contemporary Romance

Only one woman could hurt bad boy Jake Braden
Only one woman can heal him
Fiona Steele has arrived…

Fiona Steele has a great career, strong friendships, and a loving family. To an outsider, her life appears happy and fulfilling. But the one thing that's missing is true love, and the only man Fiona wants is the one she can't have, sinfully handsome and seductively intense Jake Braden—the man whose heart she broke, which she has regretted ever since.

As an LA stuntman, Jake Braden's at the top of his game. He's hired for all the best movies, hooks up with the hottest women, and lives an unencumbered lifestyle where his needs come first—and where he doesn't have to examine his life too closely. Except when he visits his family in his close-knit hometown of Trusty, Colorado, where he spends his time avoiding Fiona—the only woman who knows who he really is.

When Fiona's best friend is hired to act in Jake's movie, Fiona jumps at the chance to try to win him back. There's no denying the white-hot attraction burning between them. With every encounter, Fiona hopes Jake can't resist falling back into the love they once shared. But her well-orchestrated rendezvous doesn't go over well with the brooding heartthrob. Living in the fast lane is perfect for a guy who's buried his emotions so damn deep he's not sure he can remember how to feel—and he's not sure he ever wants to.

***Crashing Into Love***, The Bradens (Trusty, CO), Book 12
**Setting**: Hollywood, California

**Fiona Steele**
Geologist
Blue eyes, long brown hair
34

**SIBLINGS**
Reggie, Finn,
Jesse, Brent, Shea

**Jake Braden**
Stuntman
Dark eyes, dark hair
34

**SIBLINGS**
Pierce, Ross,
Wes, Emily, Luke

**PARENTS**
Catherine Braden
Buddy Walsh
(deserted family)

## CHILDREN

_____

_____

_____

_____

## BOOK ENGAGED

_____

## BOOK MARRIED

_____

## PETS

_____

## OTHER NOTES

_____

_____

_____

_____

_____

NEW YORK TIMES BESTSELLING AUTHOR

# MELISSA FOSTER

## GAME OF LOVE

{ THE REMINGTONS - DEX REMINGTON }

LOVE IN BLOOM CONTEMPORARY ROMANCE

Ellie Parker is a master at building walls around her heart. In the twenty-five years she's been alive, Dex Remington has been the only person who has always believed in her and been there for her. But four years earlier, she came to Dex seeking comfort and then disappeared like a thief in the night, leaving him a broken man.

Dex Remington is one of the top PC game developers in the United States. He's handsome, smart, and numb. So damn numb that he's not sure he'll ever find a reason to feel again.

A chance encounter sparks intense desires in Ellie and Dex. Desires that make her want to run—and make him want to feel. A combination of lust and fear leads these young lovers down a dangerous path. Is it possible to cross a burned bridge, or are they destined to be apart forever?

**Game of Love**, The Remingtons, Book 1
**Setting**: New York, New York

**Ellie Parker**
Elementary School Teacher
Baby blue eyes, dark hair
25

**Dex Remington**
Founder of
Thrive Entertainment;
Game Developer
Dark blue eyes, dark wavy hair
26

**SIBLINGS**
Jack, Rush, Kurt,
Sage, Siena

**PARENTS**
James & Joanie Remington

## CHILDREN

_____

_____

_____

_____

## BOOK ENGAGED

_____

## BOOK MARRIED

_____

## PETS

_____

## OTHER NOTES

_____

_____

_____

_____

_____

NEW YORK TIMES BESTSELLING AUTHOR

# MELISSA FOSTER

## STROKE OF
# LOVE

{ THE REMINGTONS - SAGE REMINGTON }
LOVE IN BLOOM CONTEMPORARY ROMANCE

Kate Paletto runs a volunteer program in Belize for Artists for International Aid, where she deals with self-centered artists who use the program as a means to repair their marred reputations. She loves the country, the people, and what AIA stands for, but too many diva volunteers have turned her off to press-seeking celebrities altogether and left her questioning the value of the volunteer program. When she meets incredibly handsome and charming Sage, he stirs emotions she hasn't felt for ages, even though he represents the things she despises.

Laid-back artist Sage Remington escapes his wealthy lifestyle in the Big Apple for a two-week journey of self-discovery to figure out how a guy who has so much can feel so empty. When he meets ultra-organized Kate, who lives her life the way he's always dreamed of living his, the attraction is too hot to ignore, but Sage is there to figure out what's missing in his life, not to find a woman.

Every look, and every late-night chat in the romantic jungle brings them closer together, but Sage can barely think past stripping away Kate's misconceptions about him. Kate fights him every step of the way—even though she finds it hard to ignore the strikingly handsome, generous-to-a-fault artist who wants to do nothing more than right the wrongs of the world—and love her to the ends of the earth.

### *Stroke of Love*, The Remingtons, Book 2
### **Setting**: Punta Palacia, Belize

**Kate Paletto**
Program Director,
Artists for International Aid
Blue eyes, long dark hair
26

**Sage Remington**
Artist
Blue eyes, wavy dark hair
28

**SIBLINGS**
Jack, Rush, Kurt,
Dex, Siena

**PARENTS**
James & Joanie Remington

## CHILDREN

_____

_____

_____

_____

## BOOK ENGAGED

_____

## BOOK MARRIED

_____

## PETS

_____

## OTHER NOTES

_____

_____

_____

_____

_____

NEW YORK TIMES BESTSELLING AUTHOR

# MELISSA FOSTER

## FLAMES OF LOVE

{ THE REMINGTONS - SIENA REMINGTON }

LOVE IN BLOOM CONTEMPORARY ROMANCE

As one of New York's Finest, firefighter Cash Ryder is always prepared. When a woman's car skids off the side of a mountain during a snowstorm, he's there to rescue her. Cash is totally focused on the woman's well-being, but within minutes of getting her to safety, he realizes that he's nowhere near prepared for the heat that rolls off of sensual, smart-mouthed, and stubborn Siena Remington.

As a model, Siena Remington has dated some of the wealthiest, most handsome men in the industry, and she's made peace with the idea that most men are just looking for eye candy and they wouldn't know how to romance a woman to save their lives. When she's rescued by a tall, handsome stranger, she thinks that maybe, just maybe, she's found her own real-life romantic fairy tale—until he opens his mouth and everything that comes out is gruff, ornery, and aggravatingly sexy.

Thrown together during an annual firehouse calendar photo shoot, the passion between Cash and Siena sizzles, and neither one knows how to control the flames. After an evening of verbal sparring followed by a sinfully sensual night, their darkest secrets are revealed—and so is Cash's warm, romantic heart. But Siena's secret might be too much for big, strong, always-prepared Cash to handle—and Siena is forced to choose between a man who's everything she's ever dreamed of and an opportunity of a lifetime.

**Flames of Love**, The Remingtons, Book 3
**Setting**: New York, New York

## Siena Remington
Fashion Model
Blue eyes, long brown hair
26

### SIBLINGS
Jack, Rush, Kurt,
Sage, Dex

### PARENTS
James & Joanie Remington

## Cash Ryder
Fireman
Brown eyes, dirty blond
hair
32

### SIBLINGS
Duke, Gage, Blue,
Jake, Trish

### PARENTS
Andrea & Ned Ryder

## CHILDREN

_____

_____

_____

_____

## BOOK ENGAGED

_____

## BOOK MARRIED

_____

## PETS

_____

## OTHER NOTES

_____

_____

_____

_____

_____

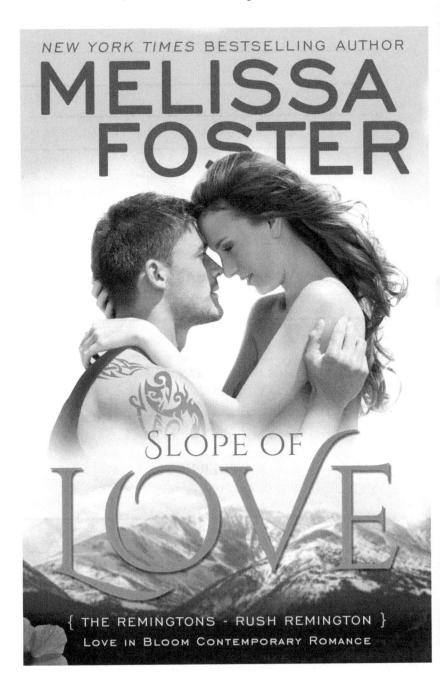

NEW YORK TIMES BESTSELLING AUTHOR

# MELISSA FOSTER

## SLOPE OF LOVE

{ THE REMINGTONS - RUSH REMINGTON }

Love in Bloom Contemporary Romance

Olympic gold medalist skiers Jayla Stone and Rush Remington have been best friends for years. They've seen each other at their best and worst and have kept each other's secrets without fail. Only there's one secret Rush has kept close to his chest. After months of introspection, Rush realizes he's been filling his bed but not tending to his heart. He's changed his womanizing ways, and the only woman who can fill his heart has been right by his side all this time.

Years of intimate conversations and the sharing of hopes and dreams collide when Rush reveals his secret, and one toe-curling kiss changes everything between Rush and Jayla. They're no match for the passion that kiss ignites, or the pull of true love. But being Rush's best friend means knowing all about his revolving bedroom door—and Jayla has a secret of her own that could jeopardize her career and her relationship with Rush. Even their love may not be enough to overcome Rush's past or secure Jayla's future.

**Slope of Love**, The Remingtons, Book 4
**Setting**: Colorado Ski Center

### Jayla Stone
Competitive Skier
Brown eyes, long brown hair
28

### SIBLINGS
Jace, Mia, Jennifer, Jared

### Rush Remington
Competitive Skier
Blue eyes, dark brown hair
32

### SIBLINGS
Jack, Kurt,
Sage, Dex, Siena

### PARENTS
James & Joanie Remington

## CHILDREN

---

---

---

---

## BOOK ENGAGED

---

## BOOK MARRIED

---

## PETS

---

## OTHER NOTES

---

---

---

---

---

NEW YORK TIMES BESTSELLING AUTHOR

# MELISSA FOSTER

## READ, WRITE, LOVE

{ THE REMINGTONS - KURT REMINGTON }

LOVE IN BLOOM CONTEMPORARY ROMANCE

Bestselling author Kurt Remington lives to write. He spends twelve hours a day in front of his computer, rarely leaving the seclusion of his beach-front property, where he's come to finish his latest thriller—that is, until free-spirited Leanna Bray nearly drowns in the ocean trying to save her dog. Kurt's best-laid plans are shot to hell when he comes to their rescue. Kurt's as irritated as he is intrigued by the sexy, hot mess of a woman who lives life on a whim, forgets everything, and doesn't even know the definition of the word organized.

Leanna's come to the Cape hoping to find a fulfilling career in the jam-making business, and until she figures out her own life, a man is not on the menu. But Leanna can't get the six-two, deliciously muscled and tragically neat Kurt out of her mind. She tells herself she's just stopping by to say thank you, but the steamy afternoon sparks a wild and sexy ride as Kurt and Leanna test the powers of Chemistry 101: Opposites Attract.

**Read, Write, Love**, The Remingtons, Book 5
**Setting**: Cape Cod & Wellfleet, Massachusetts

### Leanna Bray
Owner of
Luscious Leanna's Sweet Treats
Hazel eyes, brunette
28

### SIBLINGS
Colby, Wade,
Dae, Bailey

### PARENTS
Will & Gina Bray

### Kurt Remington
Writer
Blue eyes, dark brown hair
30

### SIBLINGS
Jack, Rush,
Sage, Dex, Siena

### PARENTS
James & Joanie Remington

*Melissa Foster*

## CHILDREN

_____

_____

_____

_____


## BOOK ENGAGED

_____


## BOOK MARRIED

_____


## PETS

_____


## OTHER NOTES

_____

_____

_____

_____

_____

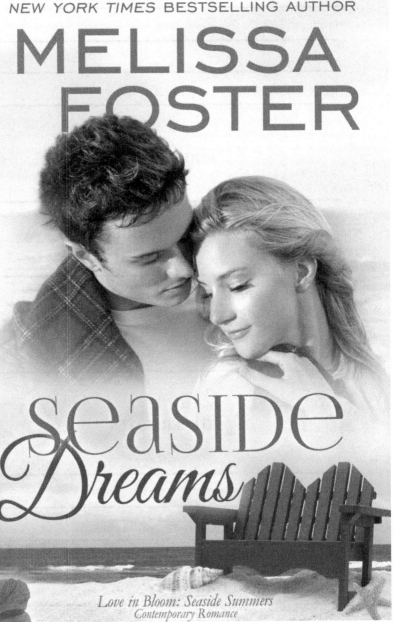

NEW YORK TIMES BESTSELLING AUTHOR

# MELISSA FOSTER

## seaside
### *Dreams*

*Love in Bloom: Seaside Summers*
Contemporary Romance

Bella Abbascia has returned to Seaside Cottages in Wellfleet, Massachusetts, as she does every summer. Only this year, Bella has more on her mind than sunbathing and skinny-dipping with her girlfriends. She's quit her job, put her house on the market, and sworn off relationships while she builds a new life in her favorite place on earth. That is, until good-time Bella's prank takes a bad turn and a sinfully sexy police officer appears on the scene.

Single father and police officer Caden Grant left Boston with his fourteen-year-old son, Evan, after his partner was killed in the line of duty. He hopes to find a safer life in the small resort town of Wellfleet, and when he meets Bella during a night patrol shift, he realizes he's found the one thing he'd never allowed himself to hope for—or even realized he was missing.

After fourteen years of focusing solely on his son, Caden cannot resist the intense attraction he feels toward beautiful Bella, and Bella's powerless to fight the heat of their budding romance. But starting over proves more difficult than either of them imagined, and when Evan gets mixed up with the wrong kids, Caden's loyalty is put to the test. Will he give up everything to protect his son—even Bella?

**Seaside Dreams**, Seaside Summers, Book 1
**Setting**: Cape Cod & Wellfleet, Massachusetts

**Bella Abbascia**
Teacher
Brown eyes, blond hair

**PARENTS**
Milton Abbascia

**Caden Grant**
Police Officer
Dark eyes, chestnut hair
35

**PARENTS**
Steven & Amber Grant

**CHILDREN**
Evan, age 14 (Caden's son)

**BOOK ENGAGED**

**BOOK MARRIED**

**PETS**

**OTHER NOTES**

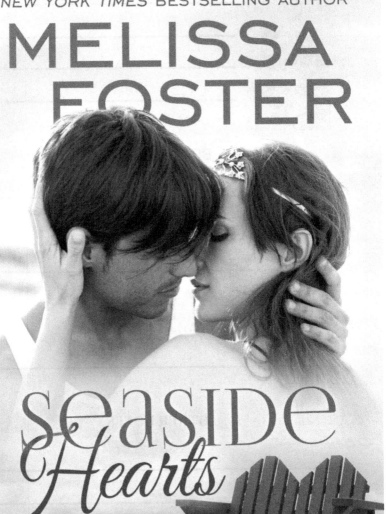

NEW YORK TIMES BESTSELLING AUTHOR

# MELISSA FOSTER

## seaside
## *Hearts*

*Love in Bloom: Seaside Summers*
Contemporary Romance

Jenna Ward is vivacious, spontaneous, and confident—except when she's around the man who stole her heart years earlier, strikingly handsome, quiet, and reliable Pete Lacroux. After years of trying to get his attention and overwhelmed from dealing with her mother's new cougar lifestyle, Jenna's giving up on Pete—and is ready to explore other men.

As the eldest of five siblings, with an alcoholic father to care for, boat craftsman Pete Lacroux always does the right thing and has no time for a real relationship. He's looking forward to seeing his friend Jenna, a welcome distraction who's so damn sexy and so painfully shy that she equally entertains and confuses him.

When Jenna picks up a hard-bodied construction worker, jealousy ignites Pete's true feelings, and he's powerless to ignore the desires for Jenna he never realized he had. But Pete's not the quiet guy he appears to be, and his life is anything but conducive to a relationship. Can Jenna handle the real Pete Lacroux—the sexiest, most passionate alpha male she's ever seen—or will she crack under pressure? And can Pete reclaim the life he once had without tearing apart his family?

**Seaside Hearts**, Seaside Summers, Book 2
**Setting**: Cape Cod & Wellfleet, Massachusetts

**Jenna Ward**
Elementary School Art Teacher
Blue eyes, brunette
29

**PARENTS**
Miranda Ward

**Pete Lacroux**
Boat Restorer;
Seaside Cottages
Maintenance Man
Blue eyes, brown hair
32

**SIBLINGS**
Hunter, Matt,
Grayson, Sky

**PARENTS**
Neil & Bea Lacroux
(mother deceased)

## CHILDREN

_____

_____

_____

_____

## BOOK ENGAGED

_____

## BOOK MARRIED

_____

## PETS

_____

## OTHER NOTES

_____

_____

_____

_____

_____

NEW YORK TIMES BESTSELLING AUTHOR

# MELISSA FOSTER

# seaside

## *Sunsets*

*Love in Bloom: Seaside Summers*
Contemporary Romance

Jessica Ayers has lived a sheltered life with little more than cello lessons and practices taking up her day. Now a member of the Boston Symphony Orchestra, she escapes the prim and proper symphony to vacation in the Seaside community in Wellfleet, Massachusetts, and determine if she is living life to the fullest or missing it altogether.

For the first time since developing the second largest search engine in the world, billionaire Jamie Reed is taking the summer off. He plans to work from the Cape and spend time with his elderly grandmother—and falling in love is not in his plans.

From the moment Jamie and Jessica meet, the attraction is white-hot. Once-overly-focused Jamie can think of little else than sensual, smart, and alluring Jessica, and Jessica discovers a side of herself she never knew existed. But when Jamie's business encounters trouble and his attorney and best friend intervenes, he proves that the brown-haired beauty is too distracting for Jamie. To make matters worse, it appears that Jessica might not be who she says she is, turning Jamie's life—and his heart—upside down. In a world where personal information is always one click away, Jamie must decide if he should trust his heart or watch the woman he loves walk away.

**Seaside Sunsets**, Seaside Summers, Book 3
**Setting**: Cape Cod, Wellfleet & Boston, Massachusetts

**Jessica Ayers**
Cellist with
Boston Symphony Orchestra
Blue eyes, light brown hair
27

**PARENTS**
Ralph & Cecilia Ayers

**Jamie Reed**
Developer of OneClick
Hazel eyes, black hair

**PARENTS**
Vera Reed, grandmother
(parents deceased)

## CHILDREN

---

---

---

---

## BOOK ENGAGED

---

## BOOK MARRIED

---

## PETS

---

## OTHER NOTES

---

---

---

---

---

NEW YORK TIMES BESTSELLING AUTHOR

# MELISSA FOSTER

## SEASIDE Secrets

*Love in Bloom: Seaside Summers*
Contemporary Romance

Tony Black is the hottest surfer on the planet. He travels the world throughout the year and spends his summers on Cape Cod with his friends, at the Seaside cottages in Wellfleet, Massachusetts. He's got his choice of women, but Amy Maples is the one he wants. Fourteen years ago she was his for an entire summer, until a devastating accident changed everything, and what they had seemed like it had never existed—at least for her.

Amy Maples is as consistent as the day is long. She's spent summers on Cape Cod forever, she always does the right thing, and she's spent years trying to reclaim the heart of Tony Black, the only man she's ever loved. She's back for a summer of fun with her friends at Seaside, only this year she's been offered the opportunity of a lifetime thousands of miles away, and she's decided to try one last time to reconnect with Tony. But having a relationship with Tony means dealing with her past—and dealing with her past may knock her to her knees.

### *Seaside Secrets*, Seaside Summers, Book 4
### Setting: Wellfleet, Massachusetts

**Amy Maples**
Owner & President of
Maples Logistical &
Conference Consulting
Green eyes, blond hair
32

**Tony Black**
Professional Surfer;
Motivational Speaker
Blue eyes, brown & blond hair
34

**PARENTS**
Jack Black (deceased)

## CHILDREN

_____

_____

_____

_____

## BOOK ENGAGED

_____

## BOOK MARRIED

_____

## PETS

_____

## OTHER NOTES

_____

_____

_____

_____

_____

NEW YORK TIMES BESTSELLING AUTHOR

# MELISSA FOSTER

# seaside

# *Nights*

*Love in Bloom: Seaside Summers*
Contemporary Romance

# BOOK SUMMARY

_____

_____

_____

_____

_____

_____

_____

_____

_____

_____

_____

_____

_____

_____

_____

_____

_____

_____

_____

_____

_____

***Seaside Nights***, Seaside Summers, Book 5
**Setting**: Wellfleet, Massachusetts

**Sky Lacroux**
Tattoo Artist
Dark hair, dark eyes
24

**SIBLINGS**
Pete, Hunter,
Matt, Grayson

**PARENTS**
Neil & Bea Lacroux
(mother deceased)

**Sawyer Bass**
Boxer; Songwriter
Dark hair, dark eyes
28

**SIBLINGS**

_____

_____

**PARENTS**
Lisa & Tad Bass

*Melissa Foster*

## CHILDREN

_____

_____

_____

_____

## BOOK ENGAGED

_____

## BOOK MARRIED

_____

## PETS

_____

## OTHER NOTES

_____

_____

_____

_____

_____

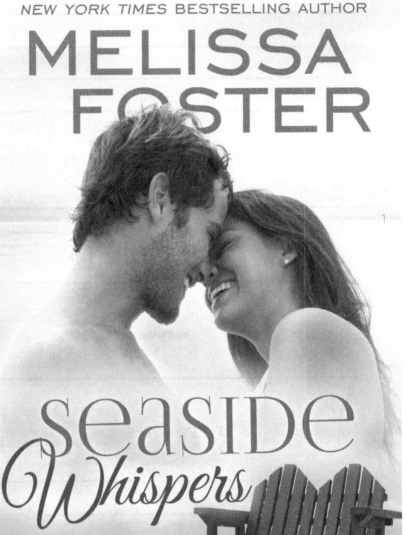

NEW YORK TIMES BESTSELLING AUTHOR

# MELISSA FOSTER

## seaside
## *Whispers*

*Love in Bloom: Seaside Summers*
Contemporary Romance

# BOOK SUMMARY

## *Seaside Whispers*, Seaside Summers, Book 6
### Setting: Wellfleet, Massachusetts

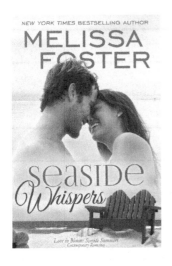

_____
_____
_____
_____

**SIBLINGS**

_____

**PARENTS**

_____

**Matt Lacroux**
Professor
Dark eyes, dark hair
30

**SIBLINGS**
Pete, Hunter,
Grayson, Sky

**PARENTS**
Neil & Bea Lacroux
(mother deceased)

*Melissa Foster*

## CHILDREN

_____

_____

_____

_____

## BOOK ENGAGED

_____

## BOOK MARRIED

_____

## PETS

_____

## OTHER NOTES

_____

_____

_____

_____

_____

NEW YORK TIMES BESTSELLING AUTHOR

# MELISSA FOSTER

## seaside Embrace

Love in Bloom: Seaside Summers
Contemporary Romance

# BOOK SUMMARY

## *Seaside Embrace*, Seaside Summers, Book 7
### Setting: Cape Cod & Boston, Massachusetts

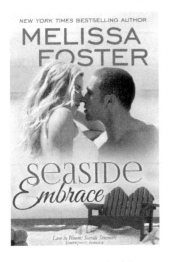

**SIBLINGS**

_____

**PARENTS**

_____

### Hunter Lacroux
Co-Owner of
Grunters Ironworks
Dark eyes, dark hair
28

### SIBLINGS
Pete, Matt,
Grayson, Sky

### PARENTS
Neil & Bea Lacroux
(mother deceased)

## CHILDREN

_____

_____

_____

_____

## BOOK ENGAGED

_____

## BOOK MARRIED

_____

## PETS

_____

## OTHER NOTES

_____

_____

_____

_____

_____

# BOOK SUMMARY

_____

_____

_____

_____

_____

_____

_____

_____

_____

_____

_____

_____

_____

_____

_____

_____

_____

_____

## *Seaside Lovers*, Seaside Summers, Book 8
### Setting: Wellfleet, Massachusetts

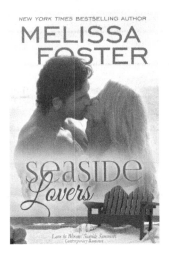

_____

_____

_____

_____

**SIBLINGS**

_____

**PARENTS**

_____

**Grayson Lacroux**
Co-Owner of
Grunters Ironworks
Dark eyes, dark hair
26

**SIBLINGS**
Pete, Hunter, Matt, Sky

**PARENTS**
Neil & Bea Lacroux
(mother deceased )

*Melissa Foster*

## CHILDREN

_____

_____

_____

_____

## BOOK ENGAGED

_____

## BOOK MARRIED

_____

## PETS

_____

## OTHER NOTES

_____

_____

_____

_____

_____

NEW YORK TIMES BESTSELLING AUTHOR

# MELISSA FOSTER

Healed By

*Love*

The Bradens

Love in Bloom: The Bradens
Contemporary Romance

Nate Braden has loved his best friend's younger sister Jewel for as long as he can remember, but between their age difference and his respect for Rick, he's always kept his feelings at bay. Now he's back in Peaceful Harbor, and Jewel is no longer sixteen years old—but there's an even bigger obstacle standing in his way. Nate and Rick joined the military together eight years earlier. Nate came home a hero, but Rick didn't make it out alive.

***Healed By Love,*** The Bradens (Peaceful Harbor), Book 1
**Setting:** Peaceful Harbor, Maryland
*Publication Order Subject To Change*

## Jewel Fisher

_____

_____

_____

### SIBLINGS

_____

_____

### PARENTS

_____

## Nate Braden

_____

_____

_____

### SIBLINGS
Cole, Sam, Tempest,
Ty, Shannon

### PARENTS
Thomas "Ace" &
Maisy Braden

## CHILDREN

_____

_____

_____

_____

## BOOK ENGAGED

_____

## BOOK MARRIED

_____

## PETS

_____

## OTHER NOTES

_____

_____

_____

_____

_____

NEW YORK TIMES BESTSELLING AUTHOR

# MELISSA FOSTER

Surrender My *Love*

The Bradens

Love in Bloom: The Bradens
Contemporary Romance

## BOOK SUMMARY

## ***Surrender My Love,*** The Bradens (Peaceful Harbor), Book 2
### Setting: Peaceful Harbor, Maryland
*Publication Order Subject To Change*

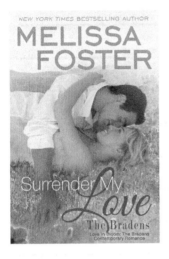

_____

_____

_____

_____

**SIBLINGS**

_____

**PARENTS**

_____

**Cole Braden**

_____

_____

_____

**SIBLINGS**
Sam, Tempest,
Nate, Ty, Shannon

**PARENTS**
Thomas "Ace" &
Maisy Braden

## CHILDREN

---

---

---

---

## BOOK ENGAGED

---

## BOOK MARRIED

---

## PETS

---

## OTHER NOTES

---

---

---

---

NEW YORK TIMES BESTSELLING AUTHOR

# MELISSA FOSTER

River of *Love*

The Bradens

Love in Bloom: The Bradens
Contemporary Romance

*Melissa Foster*

# BOOK SUMMARY

_____

_____

_____

_____

_____

_____

_____

_____

_____

_____

_____

_____

_____

_____

_____

_____

_____

_____

_____

## *River of Love,* The Bradens (Peaceful Harbor), Book 3
### Setting: Peaceful Harbor, Maryland
*Publication Order Subject To Change*

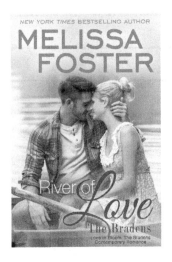

_____

_____

_____

_____

**SIBLINGS**

_____

**PARENTS**

_____

### Sam Braden
Owner of Rough Riders –
Rafting and Adventure
Company

_____

_____

### SIBLINGS
Cole, Tempest,
Nate, Ty, Shannon

### PARENTS
Thomas "Ace" & Maisy Braden

*Melissa Foster*

**CHILDREN**

_____

_____

_____

_____

**BOOK ENGAGED**

_____

**BOOK MARRIED**

_____

**PETS**

_____

**OTHER NOTES**

_____

_____

_____

_____

_____

NEW YORK TIMES BESTSELLING AUTHOR

# MELISSA FOSTER

## Crushing on *Love*

### The Bradens

Love in Bloom: The Bradens
Contemporary Romance

# BOOK SUMMARY

***Crushing on Love,*** The Bradens (Peaceful Harbor), Book 4
**Setting:** Peaceful Harbor, Maryland
*Publication Order Subject To Change*

### Shannon Braden

_____

_____

_____

### SIBLINGS
Cole, Sam, Tempest, Nate, Ty

### PARENTS
Thomas "Ace" & Maisy Braden

_____

_____

_____

### SIBLINGS

_____

_____

### PARENTS

_____

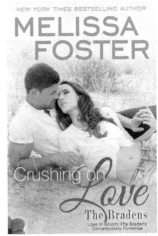

## CHILDREN

_____

_____

_____

_____

## BOOK ENGAGED

_____

## BOOK MARRIED

_____

## PETS

_____

## OTHER NOTES

_____

_____

_____

_____

_____

NEW YORK TIMES BESTSELLING AUTHOR

# MELISSA FOSTER

Whisper of
*Love*

The Bradens

Love in Bloom: The Bradens
Contemporary Romance

## BOOK SUMMARY

_____

_____

_____

_____

_____

_____

_____

_____

_____

_____

_____

_____

_____

_____

_____

_____

_____

_____

***Whisper of Love,*** The Bradens (Peaceful Harbor), Book 5
**Setting:** Peaceful Harbor, Maryland
*Publication Order Subject To Change*

### Tempest Braden
Music Therapist

_____

_____

### SIBLINGS
Cole, Sam,
Nate, Ty, Shannon

### PARENTS
Thomas "Ace" & Maisy Braden

_____

_____

_____

_____

### SIBLINGS

_____

_____

### PARENTS

_____

## CHILDREN

_____

_____

_____

_____

## BOOK ENGAGED

_____

## BOOK MARRIED

_____

## PETS

_____

## OTHER NOTES

_____

_____

_____

_____

_____

NEW YORK TIMES BESTSELLING AUTHOR

# MELISSA FOSTER

Thrill of

*Love*

The Bradens

Love in Bloom: The Bradens
Contemporary Romance

## BOOK SUMMARY

### *Thrill of Love,* The Bradens (Peaceful Harbor), Book 6
### Setting: Peaceful Harbor, Maryland
*Publication Order Subject To Change*

_____

_____

_____

_____

## SIBLINGS

_____

## PARENTS

_____

### Ty Braden
Photographer;
Mountain Climber

_____

_____

### SIBLINGS
Cole, Sam, Tempest,
Nate, Shannon

### PARENTS
Thomas "Ace" & Maisy Braden

*Melissa Foster*

## CHILDREN

_____

_____

_____

_____

## BOOK ENGAGED

_____

## BOOK MARRIED

_____

## PETS

_____

## OTHER NOTES

_____

_____

_____

_____

_____

_____

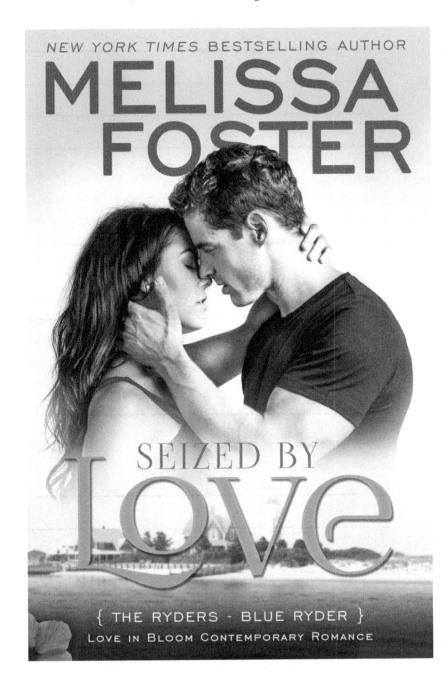

NEW YORK TIMES BESTSELLING AUTHOR

# MELISSA FOSTER

## SEIZED BY Love

{ THE RYDERS - BLUE RYDER }

LOVE IN BLOOM CONTEMPORARY ROMANCE

# BOOK SUMMARY

---

---

---

---

---

---

---

---

---

---

---

---

---

---

---

---

---

---

**_Seized By Love,_ The Ryders, Book 1**
**Setting:** _____

*Publication Order Subject To Change*

## Lizzie Barber

_____
_____
_____

### SIBLINGS

_____
_____

### PARENTS

_____

## Blue Ryder
Specialty Carpenter
Brown hair

_____
_____

### SIBLINGS
Duke, Gage,
Cash, Jake, Trish

### PARENTS
Andrea & Ned Ryder

## CHILDREN

_____

_____

_____

_____

## BOOK ENGAGED

_____

## BOOK MARRIED

_____

## PETS

_____

## OTHER NOTES

_____

_____

_____

_____

_____

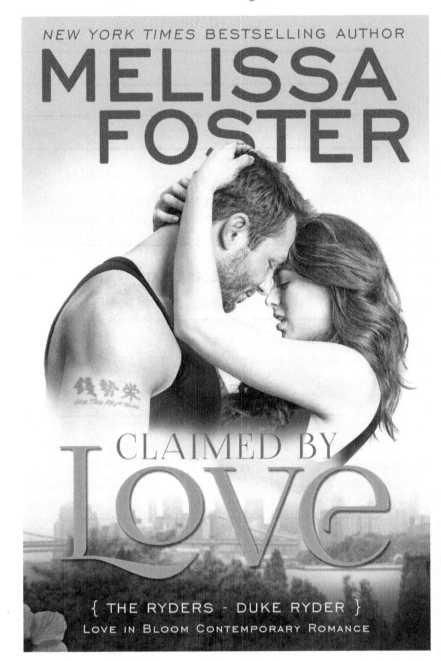

NEW YORK TIMES BESTSELLING AUTHOR

# MELISSA FOSTER

## CLAIMED BY LOVE

{ THE RYDERS - DUKE RYDER }

LOVE IN BLOOM CONTEMPORARY ROMANCE

# BOOK SUMMARY

_____

_____

_____

_____

_____

_____

_____

_____

_____

_____

_____

_____

_____

_____

_____

_____

_____

## *Claimed By Love,* The Ryders, Book 2
## Setting: _____
*Publication Order Subject To Change*

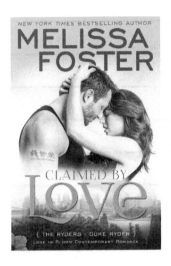

_____
_____
_____
_____

**SIBLINGS**

_____

**PARENTS**

_____

### Duke Ryder
Real Estate Investor
Dirty blond hair

_____
_____

### SIBLINGS
Gage, Blue,
Cash, Jake, Trish

### PARENTS
Andrea & Ned Ryder

## CHILDREN

---

---

---

---

## BOOK ENGAGED

---

## BOOK MARRIED

---

## PETS

---

## OTHER NOTES

---

---

---

---

---

# BOOK SUMMARY

## *Chased By Love,* The Ryders, Book 3
## Setting: _____
*Publication Order Subject To Change*

### Trish Ryder
Actress
Hazel eyes

---

### SIBLINGS
Duke, Gage, Blue, Cash, Jake

### PARENTS
Andrea & Ned Ryder

### Boone Stryker
Musician

---

---

### SIBLINGS

---

### PARENTS

---

## CHILDREN

_____

_____

_____

_____

## BOOK ENGAGED

_____

## BOOK MARRIED

_____

## PETS

_____

## OTHER NOTES

_____

_____

_____

_____

_____

NEW YORK TIMES BESTSELLING AUTHOR

# MELISSA FOSTER

## SWEPT INTO Love

{ THE RYDERS - GAGE RYDER }

LOVE IN BLOOM CONTEMPORARY ROMANCE

# BOOK SUMMARY

## *Swept Into Love,* The Ryders, Book 4
### Setting: Allure, Colorado
*Publication Order Subject To Change*

**Sally Tuft**
Accounting & Scheduling at
No Limitz Youth Center
Blue eyes, white, blond hair

**SIBLINGS**

_____

**PARENTS**

_____

**Gage Ryder**
Sports Director at
NoLimitz Youth Center
Blue eyes, sandy blond hair

**SIBLINGS**
Duke, Blue,
Cash, Jake, Trish

**PARENTS**
Andrea & Ned Ryder

## CHILDREN

---

---

---

---

## BOOK ENGAGED

---

## BOOK MARRIED

---

## PETS

---

## OTHER NOTES

---

---

---

---

---

NEW YORK TIMES BESTSELLING AUTHOR

# MELISSA FOSTER

## RESCUED BY LOVE

{ THE RYDERS - JAKE RYDER }

LOVE IN BLOOM CONTEMPORARY ROMANCE

*Melissa Foster*

# BOOK SUMMARY

_____

_____

_____

_____

_____

_____

_____

_____

_____

_____

_____

_____

_____

_____

_____

_____

_____

_____

_____

_____

_____

_____

**Rescued By Love,** The Ryders, Book 5
**Setting:** _____
*Publication Order Subject To Change*

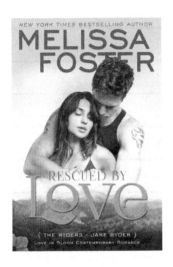

**SIBLINGS**

_____

**PARENTS**

_____

**Jake Ryder**
Army Ranger;
Mountain Rescue Specialist

_____
_____

**SIBLINGS**
Duke, Gage, Blue,
Cash, Trish

**PARENTS**
Andrea & Ned Ryder

*Melissa Foster*

## CHILDREN

_____

_____

_____

_____

## BOOK ENGAGED

_____

## BOOK MARRIED

_____

## PETS

_____

## OTHER NOTES

_____

_____

_____

_____

_____

# Full LOVE IN BLOOM SERIES order

Love in Bloom books may be read as stand alones. For more enjoyment, read them in series order. Characters from each series carry forward to the next.

### SNOW SISTERS
Sisters in Love
Sisters in Bloom
Sisters in White

### THE BRADENS (Weston, CO)
Lovers at Heart
Destined for Love
Friendship on Fire
Sea of Love
Bursting with Love
Hearts at Play

### THE BRADENS (Trusty, CO)
Taken by Love
Fated for Love
Romancing my Love
Flirting with Love
Dreaming of Love
Crashing into Love

### THE BRADENS (Peaceful Harbor, MD)
(Coming Soon)
Healed by Love
Surrender My Love
River of Love
Crushing on Love
Whisper of Love
Thrill of Love

## BRADEN WORLD NOVELLAS
Daring Her Love (1001 Dark Nights)
Promise My Love

## THE REMINGTONS
Game of Love
Stroke of Love
Flames of Love
Slope of Love
Read, Write, Love

## SEASIDE SUMMERS
Seaside Dreams
Seaside Hearts
Seaside Sunsets
Seaside Secrets
(Coming Soon)
Seaside Nights
Seaside Whispers
Seaside Embrace
Seaside Lovers

*Publication order subject to change without notice*

## THE RYDERS
(Coming Soon)
Seized by Love
Claimed by Love
Chased by Love
Swept Into Love
Rescued by Love

## MORE LOVE IN BLOOM BOOKS
(Coming Soon)
THE STEELES
THE STONES
THE BRAYS

## WILD BOYS AFTER DARK
Logan
Heath
Jackson
Cooper

## BAD BOYS AFTER DARK
Dylan
Mick
Carson
Brett

## HARBORSIDE NIGHTS
Includes characters from
Love in Bloom series

Catching Cassidy
Discovering Delilah
(Coming Soon)
Tempting Tristan
Chasing Charley
Breaking Brandon
Embracing Evan
Reaching Rusty
Loving Livi

*Melissa Foster*

**SIGN UP for MELISSA'S NEWSLETTER to stay up to date with new releases, giveaways, and events**

NEWSLETTER:
http://www.melissafoster.com/newsletter

## CONNECT WITH MELISSA

TWITTER:
https://twitter.com/Melissa_Foster

FACEBOOK:
https://www.facebook.com/MelissaFosterAuthor

WEBSITE:
http://www.melissafoster.com

STREET TEAM:
http://www.facebook.com/groups/melissafosterfans

Melissa Foster is a *New York Times* and *USA Today* bestselling and award-winning author. Her books have been recommended by *USA Today's* book blog, *Hagerstown* magazine, *The Patriot*, and several other print venues. She is the founder of the World Literary Café, and when she's not writing, Melissa helps authors navigate the publishing industry through her author training programs on Fostering Success. Melissa also hosts Aspiring Authors contests for children and has painted and donated several murals to the Hospital for Sick Children in Washington, DC.

Visit Melissa on her website or chat with her on social media. Melissa enjoys discussing her books with book clubs and reader groups and welcomes an invitation to your event.

Melissa's books are available through most online retailers in paperback and digital formats.